TWO THAT
WERE TOUGH

Also by Robert Burch

D. J.'S WORST ENEMY

DOODLE AND THE GO-CART

HUT SCHOOL AND THE WARTIME
HOME-FRONT HEROES

JOEY'S CAT

QUEENIE PEAVY

RENFROE'S CHRISTMAS

SIMON AND THE GAME OF CHANCE

SKINNY

TYLER, WILKIN, AND SKEE

TWO THAT WERE TOUGH

Robert Burch

Illustrated by Richard Cuffari

THE VIKING PRESS · NEW YORK

FIRST EDITION
TEXT COPYRIGHT © ROBERT BURCH, 1976
ILLUSTRATIONS COPYRIGHT © VIKING PENGUIN INC., 1976
ALL RIGHTS RESERVED
FIRST PUBLISHED IN 1976 BY THE VIKING PRESS
625 MADISON AVENUE, NEW YORK, N.Y. 10022
PUBLISHED SIMULTANEOUSLY IN CANADA BY
THE MACMILLAN COMPANY OF CANADA LIMITED
PRINTED IN U.S.A.
1 2 3 4 5 80 79 78 77 76
LIBRARY OF CONGRESS CATALOGING IN PUBLICATION DATA
BURCH, ROBERT, 1925—   TWO THAT WERE TOUGH.
SUMMARY: AN OLD MAN AND A WILD GRAY CHICKEN SURVIVE
THE YEARS, EACH VALUING HIS FREEDOM ABOVE ALL ELSE.
[1. OLD AGE—FICTION.   2. CHICKENS—FICTION]
I. CUFFARI, RICHARD, 1925–   II. TITLE.
PZ7.B91585TW   [FIC]   76-12453
ISBN 0-670-73684-8

For my brother, GRAHAM, and HIS FAMILY,
and OUR KIN who descended from WILLIAM BENNETT—
a great-great-grandfather
who built a gristmill

Contents

TWO THAT
WERE TOUGH

1

Hatched
in the Briers

At the York farm there were wooden nests with straw in them, where the hens laid their eggs. But one hen was not like the others. She was bigger than they were, and she could fly higher and farther. She belonged to the Yorks, but she laid her eggs in the wild. Her nest was not even on the farm. It was across the road in the mulberry thicket near the Hilton gristmill.

When she had laid thirteen eggs, the hen began to set on them. Once each day she left her stolen nest to search for food.

"That's a wild one!" said Mrs. York. "She's part game and part Leghorn, and part who knows what."

Her husband laughed. "Part eagle or hawk!" he said, watching the hen half-run, half-fly down the long driveway. She had stayed in the yard just long enough to eat the table scraps Mrs. York had thrown out.

At her nest, surrounded by briers, the hen settled onto her eggs again to keep them warm. She did not cluck over them. Her eggs could hatch or they couldn't; she was not going to make a fuss about it.

At the end of three weeks nine of the eggs hatched. The hen led her chicks into the warm, spring sunshine. If she heard the peeping sound that came from one of the eggs still in the nest, it did not stop her from leaving.

The hen walked slowly along the edge of the millpond toward the gristmill. She pecked about for cracked grain and bits of corn meal that had been spilled on the ground in front of it. She stayed there with her chicks all afternoon, but she did not cluck noisily the way other hens might, urging her little ones to eat. They could eat or they couldn't; it was up to them.

Mr. Hilton sat on a bench near the doorway of his mill and watched the hen and her brood. He had grown up in the cottage at the head of the pond, and his mother had kept a flock of chickens. Any eggs that were not used by the family were sold to the storekeeper in town. The "egg money" was spending money for the mother and the boy, and whenever hens stole their nests it was the boy's job to find them.

Mr. Hilton thought back on those days. He had known the pond and the woods around it better than any chicken. Well, he had to admit that occasionally a hen outwitted him and kept her nest hidden until the day she appeared in the open with a brand-new family. There was something special about a brood of baby chicks. He smiled as he thought of his father, who had been the miller ahead of him. He always made certain that a bit of meal or grain spilled onto the ground whenever there was a need for it.

Near sundown the hen led her chicks back into the mulberry thicket. At the nest, in addition to three eggs that would never hatch, there was a gray chick. Only half-dried, it shivered in the late afternoon coolness. The hen pecked at it as if she wanted to drive it away, but when the other chicks gathered onto the nest, the hen settled over them and provided warmth for all.

For two days the hen kept her family near the mulberry thicket, leading the chicks no farther than the clearing by the mill for food and the edge of the pond for water. Then, on the third day, she set out on a longer journey.

She crossed to the other side of the road. The chicks hurried after her, tumbling over one another as they tried to keep up. She did not cluck or seem to care whether they got across the road safely. They could make it or they couldn't.

One of them did not make it. A car came around the

curve and killed a chick just as the brood was almost to the other side. The hen did not look back. She led the way into the Yorks' farmyard. She and the remaining chicks drank the extra buttermilk from each day's churning, which Mrs. York poured into an old skillet. Next the brood ate bread crumbs tossed to them from the kitchen window. When Mrs. York walked into the yard, the chicks scurried away from her. The gray one was the most cautious. He dashed under the house and did not return until the farmer's wife was gone.

During the rest of spring the hen and her chicks spent part of their time near the gristmill and part of it across the road in the farmyard. They traveled back and forth a number of times every day. One more chick was killed while trying to cross the road.

Another drowned after she had chased a mosquito onto the end of the dam and fallen into the pond. The dam held back the water that turned the wheel that ran the gristmill.

The dam and the gristmill, with its big wheel, were at one end of the pond. At the other end, some distance away, through a grove of big trees, was Mr. Hilton's cottage. Behind it a fast-flowing stream widened to become the head of the pond. The yard of the mill was clear except for the mulberry thicket, but across the pond there were dense woods. Below the dam there were trees and wild flowers where the flow of water became a stream once more and went on about its way.

By early summer the chicks had grown wing feathers and could fly, and all except the gray one began roosting in the hen house. He flew into a dogwood tree just outside the hen house and spent the first night there. The next afternoon he did not return to the farmyard. He went to roost in a sapling in the mulberry thicket. The following night he slept in a pine tree in the grove.

When the chicks were half-grown, Mrs. York spoke of them as "frying size." One morning she stood at the back steps and dropped bits of cornbread and biscuits at her feet. Every chicken in the flock gathered close to her—except the gray one, who stood back. Then, while the chickens were busy eating, Mrs. York took a wire hook she had made from a coathanger and reached out and caught a chicken by one of his feet. She snatched him from the ground and soon had a firm grasp on him with both hands. He squawked loudly, and the other chickens flew away, cackling.

The chicken that had been caught was never seen again. For several days afterward the others were leery of Mrs. York. Then they dared go close to her again—lured by crumbs.

The only chicken that did not fall for the trick was the gray one. Instead of waiting for handouts he searched for his own food. There was grain near the gristmill and worms in the ground, berries at the edge of the grove between the gristmill and the cottage, and grass along the roadside.

These things had to be hunted, and the gray chicken stayed busy foraging from early morning till nightfall. He went into the farmyard only when grain at the mill was in short supply or the ground so dry that worms burrowed too deep to be scratched out. Even then the chicken stayed away from the back steps.

By fall the gray chicken was almost grown. He was tall and lean, with slate-colored feathers that shone like satin. His legs and wings were longer and stronger than any other chicken's in the flock, even the biggest rooster's, and he could run faster and fly higher and farther.

One day two teenage boys camped in the grove. They saw the chicken at dusk, scratching for grubs in a rotted stump. "Let's catch it," said one of the boys.

"And use it for turtle bait!" said the other. "You slip around from the other side, and I'll ease up on it from here. I'll give a signal when it's time to pounce!"

As silently as Indian scouts the boys made their way

through the trees, and the gray chicken did not see them. Then, when the boys were almost to the stump, the first one gave the signal. They jumped. The chicken sprang into the air between them. He spread his wings and flew into the treetops. From one top branch he flew to another, and then another, until he was far from the two campers.

The gray chicken roosted higher than usual in the trees that night. The next day, when the boys were gone, he was back at the rotted stump. He pecked about for grubs as calmly as if his life had never been in danger.

2

Worms That Cost a Dime Apiece

Aғтᴇʀ harvest Mr. York told Mr. Hilton, "We're moving away."

"Are you taking your farm with you?" asked Mr. Hilton.

Mr. York laughed. "No, we'll buy one in the southern part of the state, where fields are bigger and flatter and easier to plow. Big tractors need turning-around space."

Mr. Hilton looked at the cropland across the road, much of it in small patches on a hillside. "Yep, land hereabouts was meant to be worked by men and mules instead of machinery. All the same, I hate to see you go. You're my only neighbors."

"Better join us!" said the farmer. "Come on and move with us."

"No, thanks," said Mr. Hilton. "These red clay hills are my home. Why, I've never spent even one night anywhere else."

"Not even when you got married?" asked Mr. York.

"Nope, not even then. Me and Janie got married in town late one Saturday afternoon after I closed the mill, and we came on home for supper. My folks had died in the flu epidemic earlier that year, and warn't nobody else here to take care of things. But tell me, what's to become of the farm?"

"A family in Atlanta bought it."

"Will they move in right away? I hope they've got a passel of children."

"They're not planning to live here for a while," said the farmer.

"Why, the place'll grow up!"

Mr. York shook his head. "I know, but they plan to let it go wild. Oh, I suppose someday they'll want a garden or a little watermelon patch. They plan to move down here in a year or two when their children are a bit older."

Mr. Hilton smiled. "Kids'll liven us up!" he said. His children, a son and daughter, were both grown and had children of their own. Even some of his grandchildren were grown now and starting their own families. Occasionally some of them came to see him, but it wasn't like old times when Mildred and Henry and their friends had played around the gristmill and in the grove of big trees— or when his grandchildren were young and Janie was living. The kids would come and stay all summer then. They swam in the pond and played in an old boat that he kept in those days. Down below the dam, in the shallow water, they seined for fish but caught tadpoles instead, and in the grove they chased chipmunks and squirrels but never caught

[13]

one. He could hear them whooping and hollering, having themselves a good time. Nowadays the only kids he saw were picnickers in the summer, but they were different. He didn't get to know them by name, and they never wanted to hear ghost stories or tales about old times.

A few days before the Yorks were to move, Mrs. York caught her chickens. She simply closed the door of the hen house after they had gone to roost, and they were caught— all except the gray one. He was perched high in a sweet gum tree across the road.

Every day afterward Mrs. York tried to catch him. She would go into the yard, biscuits in her apron pocket, and call loudly, "*Chick-oop! Chick-chick-chick-oop!*"

Her husband teased her: "Maybe you've got a talent for hog calling too!"

She did not think it was funny. "I want the gray chicken!" she said between clenched teeth. Then she called again, "*Chick-oop! Chick-chick-chick-oop!*" tossing bread crumbs onto the ground.

The gray chicken was chasing a cricket near the end of the long driveway. He heard her call and went near the house. When the woman had returned to the kitchen, he walked into the yard and ate crumbled biscuits. Afterward he went back and tried again to catch the cricket.

In the morning the farmer and his wife moved away. When the heavy truck turned onto the highway and headed south, the gray chicken was out by the roadside, pecking at kudzu leaves. The chickens of the farm flock were in a box near the tailgate. They cackled frantically, and the gray chicken stood and listened till they were out of sight; then he walked toward the millpond.

That afternoon a man caught a fish that was bigger than any he had ever seen. The fisherman was so excited about his catch that he hurried to the gristmill to show it to Mr.

[15]

Hilton. While he was gone, the gray chicken discovered the carton of bait worms. He pecked at the carton until it turned over, and scratched at the big lump of wriggling worms. Soon he had eaten every one of them.

Meanwhile, Mr. Hilton looked at the fish the man had caught. "I've never seen one bigger," he said. "What's your secret?"

"It's the worms I use," said the man. "They're a special kind that are shipped here from Louisiana. I bought them at the bait shop in town, and they cost a dime apiece. But they're worth every cent of it!" Then he hurried out. "Maybe I'll catch another one!" he called to Mr. Hilton.

In less than five minutes he was back. His face was red, and he sounded hysterical. He screamed so loudly that Mr. Hilton was afraid the man had been bitten by one of the moccasins that sometimes sunned themselves at the water's edge. At last the man calmed down enough to explain what had happened. A big gray chicken had turned over the bait carton and eaten all of his worms—the special ones that had been shipped from Louisiana and cost a dime apiece. "You ought to get rid of that critter!" he complained.

"It's none of mine," said Mr. Hilton. "Kill it if you want to!" The man was so mad that he went chasing after the chicken, waving his fishing rod in the air.

The chicken flew into a clump of mulberry saplings. The fisherman went in after him. The chicken came out the other side. With his wings outspread, he ran to the narrow part of the pond. Then he flapped his wings and soared through the air to the opposite bank.

For the rest of the afternoon the chicken strolled about in tall grass, pecking at seed pods and looking out occasionally to see what was happening across the pond. He could see the man in the mulberry thicket, trying to untangle his fishing line, which was caught in the briers.

3

The Ice Storm

FINDING food was not easy for the chicken that winter. There were dried seeds, but the birds had eaten most of them, and now and then there were table scraps near the miller's cottage. There was nothing to eat in the farmyard now. The old skillet, where Mrs. York had poured the extra buttermilk, was full of dead leaves. And, of course, there was no more crumbled bread. Sometimes the chicken scratched around the back steps as if a crumb might be turned up, but most of his time was spent near the gristmill. Bits of grain were his main source of life in the dead of winter.

One afternoon in late February a man brought corn for Mr. Hilton to grind. His son and daughter were with him, and the boy and girl watched the machinery running. Mr. Hilton explained to them how the giant millstones ground the corn. He gave them a sample of meal so freshly ground that it was still warm. "Taste it!" he told them.

"It smells good!" said the girl.

"It *is* good!" said the boy, barely touching his tongue to the meal. Then they went outside to play. Soon they were back inside, asking about the gray chicken they'd seen eating grain that had spilled onto the ground.

"What kind of chicken is it?" asked the boy.

"It's a mill chicken," said Mr. Hilton.

"Is it yours?" asked the girl.

"It's *yours* if you can catch it," said the miller, and the girl and her brother ran outside again.

When the corn had been ground and the bags of meal were ready to be taken home, the man called his children.

"Is that chicken a rooster?" asked the boy, getting into his father's pickup truck.

"I never heard it crow," said Mr. Hilton.

"Then it must be a hen," said the girl.

"If it has ever laid an egg, I don't know about it," said Mr. Hilton, and the boy and girl looked puzzled as the truck drove away.

That night a cold drizzle turned into ice by morning, and the ground was frozen over. Roads would be too slippery for anyone to come to the gristmill, so the miller stayed in his cottage. He wished he had bought more supplies the last time he'd gone to town.

For breakfast he ate a dish of cold cereal, and his lunch was crackers and a can of Vienna sausages—the last one on the kitchen shelf. His daughter, Mildred, was always scolding him for not eating properly. She wanted him to move to Atlanta and live with her and her husband, or to

Richmond and live with his son, Henry. Mildred argued that the mill did not do enough business to bother keeping it open. Mr. Hilton had to admit that she was right. But still, he did not want to leave the mill or his cottage.

In the late afternoon he saw the chicken in his backyard. Well, there would be no scraps today, he thought, but it worried him when he realized that the gray chicken probably had not eaten anything all day. The bits of spilled grain in front of the mill were under a layer of ice.

In the cupboard Mr. Hilton found two slices of a pound cake that Mildred had sent him. He ate one slice and took the other to the back door. The steps would be slippery, he knew, and he had promised Mildred that he would not leave the cottage when ice was on the ground. If he slipped and broke a bone, he would have to go and live with Mildred or Henry for certain—or maybe to a nursing home. Mr. Hilton crumbled the cake and threw it into the yard. Then he went back inside and looked out the window.

, After the chicken had eaten the cake, he drank water from a melting icicle. At dusk he flew onto the little porch at the front of the house. For the first time ever he sought more protection from the cold than the branches of a pine tree.

"Now you know about ice storms!" said Mr. Hilton, as if the chicken could hear him. The chicken looked cold, and Mr. Hilton wished he hadn't torn down the old coop in his yard. It would have been a good shelter for a night like this. "You could go up to the farmyard and roost in the hen house," he said, watching the chicken jump onto a beam that was higher up. "But something might get you!" He supposed that somehow the chicken realized it was safer to be near human beings than far away from them —even if the only human being to be near was a tired old man.

Mr. Hilton smiled. He and the chicken were alike in some ways, he told himself. Both were alone, and both were happy to be free. "I'd open the door and invite you inside," he said, "but you'd fly away!" He went across and poked at the log, his last one, that was burning in the fireplace. "And, anyway, old Wild Wings," he called back in the direction of the porch, "you've got feathers! Maybe they'll keep you from freezing!"

4

The Picnic

In a day's time the ice had melted, and there were no more bad storms. Cool days turned into warm ones, and new life appeared everywhere. Vegetables grew in the miller's garden, and grass and weeds sprang up by the pond. The worms were just under the soil, insects on the ground, in it, and over it, and tadpoles at the water's edge. Living became easier for Mr. Hilton and Wild Wings. Best of all, for both of them, warm weather brought out picnickers.

Mr. Hilton never charged anyone for using the pond or the grove, and often people thanked him by inviting him for lunch. If he declined, they would bring him a paper plate piled high with sandwiches and potato chips, deviled eggs and pickles, cake and cookies. And afterward there were scraps, and Wild Wings would have a picnic too.

One July afternoon a group of children and women arrived from town. "We're entertaining the boys and girls in our Sunday school class," explained one of the women.

"Glad to have you here!" said Mr. Hilton. "Enjoy yourselves!" The woman went back to where the children were unloading a small aluminum boat strapped to the top of a car.

Soon the boat was in the water, and the children took turns rowing it around the pond. The women stayed on the bank and called to them, "Be careful, do you hear?" "Don't anybody drown!" Everyone was busy taking turns riding in the boat or reminding those in it to be careful. Between rides the boys and girls skipped stones, chased each other along the water's edge—and threw dabs of mud at each other when the grownups weren't looking.

While the children were having their fun, the gray chicken, who had learned to look for scraps in the parking area, discovered the picnic baskets on a table. He flew onto the table and looked cautiously at the food. When he finally pecked at a piece of wax paper, pimento cheese sandwiches were uncovered. Wild Wings ate the corner off one of them. Next he scratched at the side of the basket and with his strong claws and long legs turned the basket over. For half an hour he scratched and pecked, scratched and pecked, scattering the lunch over the table and onto the ground. He ate only a little of the food, but he ate a little bit, or a a litle bite, from every sandwich. He also sampled the sweets, taking a chunk from a slice of cake here and a cookie there. When he came to a batch of raisin cupcakes, he tore into them excitedly, pecking at the raisins as if they were juicy bugs that might get away if they were not eaten in a hurry.

At five o'clock the children docked the boat. "It's time to eat!" said one of the women.

"You don't have to beg us!" said the biggest boy. "We're starved!"

"Us too!" shouted the girls, and they raced the boys to the picnic table.

Wild Wings was on the ground when the children spotted him, eating dry-roasted peanuts from a broken jar, which had landed on a rock. "Hey!" yelled one of the boys. "A chicken's in our lunch!"

"The food's all over the place!" shouted a girl.

"Oh, my!" said the first woman to get there, and while she looked at the mess, the children—eleven girls and ten boys—decided to catch the gray chicken. They surrounded him, and when they gathered in closer, Wild Wings flew over them and into the mulberry thicket. The children dashed into the thicket after him. The chicken flew out the other side, and the children raced out too. At the narrow part of the pond Wild Wings soared into the air and flew across to the opposite bank.

"Quick, let's go after it!" shouted one of the girls. She pushed the boat back into the water, and everybody tried to get into it at the same time. It sank in the shallow water, but the children had it afloat again soon. Then they organized themselves so that a few at a time could paddle to the opposite shore. There they waited quietly so that the chicken, pecking about in the grassy strip below them, would not suspect that the chase was still on. When all but the teachers were across the pond, the children fanned out in every direction, and Wild Wings flew into the woods back of the grassy strip. The children went in after him. The teachers, across the pond, called to them, "Come back, children! Those woods are dangerous!" and "There's a swamp farther on, do you hear?" If the boys and girls heard, they were too excited to give up now, and the warnings became more and more distant and eventually faded away.

The chase continued till sundown. There were so many

children in pursuit that someone always had the chicken in view. "Here it is!" one would call, and everyone else would gather around.

If Wild Wings had flown into a tree, he rested for a few moments as if he were waiting for all the children. Then someone would either climb the tree or throw a stone, and Wild Wings would leave his perch and the chase would begin again.

Sometimes Wild Wings flew into another tree, and sometimes he returned to the ground and ran along the forest floor. Always he went deeper and deeper into the woods, and always the children raced after him.

Gradually the woods began to change. There were fewer big trees but more smaller ones. The undergrowth grew thicker, making it hard to see. Big patches of briers had to be gone around. The boys and girls lost sight of the chicken, and as darkness closed in they began to lose sight of each other.

At the gristmill a group of men from town, mostly fathers of the children, formed a search party. With flashlights and lanterns they went through the woods and into the swamp.

By midnight all the boys and girls had been led back to safety. They were scratched and bruised, and some of them were angry. "It was the chicken's fault," said a girl.

"Well, it sure knows it got run off!" said one of the boys. He turned to Mr. Hilton and added, "That gray chicken's gone! It's so far from here it won't ever find its way home." But in the morning Wild Wings was back at the picnic tables, scratching at cupcake crumbs and pecking at raisins.

5

The Close Call

Pᴵɴᴱ trees began to grow in the farmer's field across the road. "It doesn't take long for a farm to go back to a wild state," said Mr. Hilton.

"How long since that one was worked?" asked his visitor, loading flour into the trunk of his car.

"Three years now. Folks keep moving off the farms hereabouts."

"The way Atlanta's growing," said the man, "we're gonna be suburbs instead of farm country before you know it, and people will be moving back into this area."

"I'll be glad to have neighbors," said Mr. Hilton. "But if none of them grow wheat or corn I'll be out of business. Why, you're the only customer I've had today!" He didn't tell the man that he hadn't had even one customer the day before.

"I suppose gristmills are just about a thing of the past," said the man. "But I still like to grow my own grain and have it ground."

"I hear that a lot of young people feel the way you do," said Mr. Hilton. "Maybe someday this old mill will do a brisk business again. I'd like to think it'd still be in operation when I'm dead and gone."

"Folks'll always have to eat," said the man.

Mr. Hilton, of course, had to eat too, but the older he got the less he worried about it.

During the growing season he still had a small garden. When Janie was alive, she had canned vegetables, but now

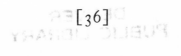

he depended on store-bought food during winter. Sometimes he closed the mill for an afternoon and went into town to stock up on supplies. Mildred often asked him if he ate a balanced diet. She always asked it as if she were certain that he did not, and he would tell her that he managed to stay healthy. And somehow he did manage to stay healthy —until he caught the flu.

It was during a snowstorm, the worst one Georgia had ever had, and Mr. Hilton came down with a high fever. He ached all over, and he slept for two days. When the snow began to melt, the weather turned bitterly cold, and the melting snow turned to ice. One morning just as day was breaking, Mr. Hilton opened his eyes. There, just outside his window, on a low limb of a tree, the gray chicken was perched, looking in at him. Mr. Hilton closed his eyes. When he opened them again, the chicken was still there. He probably hadn't had anything to eat all week, thought Mr. Hilton. Feebly he got up and made his way to the kitchen, where he found a piece of bread and a small package of crackers. After he had crumbled the bread and crackers, he tossed them outside and then heated himself some canned soup and made a pot of coffee. He wished he had saved some of the crackers to go with the soup, but it was too late now. He smiled as he watched the chicken eating the crumbs. When they were gone, Wild Wings attempted to scratch the icy ground as if more crumbs might turn up.

The ice melted during the day, and the next morning Mildred came from Atlanta. When she found out that her father was sick, she went into town for medicine and food and telephoned her family that she would stay for a few days.

She pleaded with Mr. Hilton to move to Atlanta. "You had a close call," she said. "What if I hadn't come along?"

Her father admitted that he was not as strong as he once was. "But I'm not giving up!" he said firmly. "Maybe I haven't looked after myself as well as I should, but I'll do better now that I'm well again."

On the day Mildred was to go back to Atlanta, Mr. Hilton had a relapse, and she stayed longer. When he was better, she tried once more to persuade him to move to the city. He was too weak to put up a strong argument, and one day when he had run out of other reasons to give her for not moving away, he happened to see the gray chicken. Wild Wings was scratching at a pile of leaves and acorns in the grove. Mr. Hilton pointed at him. "There!" he said. "There's another reason I can't leave here! Who'd look after the chicken?"

"It's a wild thing and could look after itself," said his daughter.

"No," said Mr. Hilton, "it's like me and needs some help. If we were like squirrels and gathered nuts for the winter, we might do better—the chicken and me!"

Mildred laughed. "Maybe you should hibernate like bears."

"Or fly south in cold weather like wild geese," said Mr. Hilton. "They have the right idea!"

"But since you're not a squirrel or a bear or a wild goose, you must move to the city with me."

"I can't do it. I can't leave the chicken."

"Oh, all right," said his daughter, and he was pleased. He'd won the argument—or thought he had until she added, "You can bring the chicken with you."

"To Atlanta?" he asked, half-shouting it as if the idea were the most preposterous thing he'd ever heard.

"Some of the kids in my neighborhood were given Easter chickens last year, and they still have them. My next-door neighbor has two of them that her grandchildren keep as pets in a pen. We'll smuggle the mill chicken into the city and build a coop for it in our yard. It'll be fed and sheltered."

"The same as me," said Mr. Hilton under his breath, and suddenly he felt too tired to argue. He promised Mildred that if she would leave him alone about it now that spring was due, he would come and live with her the following winter.

A few days after Mildred had gone home and he was by himself in the cottage, Mr. Hilton woke up at midnight. The house was light, and he believed day was breaking. Then he realized that the light came from the full moon outside. The branches on the trees in the grove were bare at this time of year, and the gristmill could be seen through them. The pond reflected moonlight like a giant mirror. "Yeah, but you're giving it up!" said a voice in the back of his head.

"Not till next winter," he answered, "and next winter is a year away! I'll wait and worry about it then." He had turned over to go back to sleep when suddenly there was a loud squawking noise. He sat up and looked outside. Feathers were drifting past the window, and the gray chicken was flying from the porch into a tree across the yard. Mr. Hilton saw a fox slink down the steps and around the corner of the house.

In the morning warm sunshine signaled the coming of spring, and Mr. Hilton sat on a bench in front of the mill.

Wild Wings was out near the mulberries, and Mr. Hilton called to him, "You almost got caught last night, didn't you? You had a close call!"

The chicken looked up as if he didn't care to be reminded of what had happened. "In your younger days *nothing* could have slipped up on you," continued Mr. Hilton. "You're failing. Why, you must be about as old for a chicken as I am for a man!"

Wild Wings turned and started away. Mr. Hilton laughed. "Don't worry," he called, "those tail feathers'll grow back—unless the fox gets all of you next time!"

6

The Feast

No sooner had the chicken's tail feathers grown back than it was fall again. Mr. Hilton wished he had not promised to move to Atlanta. There had been a spring, of course, a brief one with warm days and cool nights, followed by summer. Good weather had brought out fishermen, picnickers, and a few customers. There had not been as many customers as in the days when Mr. Hilton had sometimes had to run the mill late into the night, but there were more than the year before. "Maybe folks really are growing their own food again," he told Mildred in mid-September. He hoped she would want him to keep the mill open for another year at least, but she would not let him go back on his promise: he was to move to the city by winter. Well, fall was just beginning. Maybe it would last a while, but he doubted it.

He supposed that time moved along in no more of a hurry than it had during his youth; it only seemed that it did. When he was a boy, playing in the woods or helping his father at the mill, a day was a long and wonderful thing. "A day is still a wonderful thing," he said to himself, looking at the colors in the autumn sunset, "but there hasn't been one in years that's been long enough!" Wild Wings was perched on an old sawhorse nearby, and Mr. Hilton called to him, "I know! It's me that's not the same. Well, you don't get any younger either!"

In early October things began to happen at the farmhouse across the road. First, loads of lumber and other building supplies were hauled up the long driveway and piled in the yard. Then carpenters arrived. Mr. Hilton could hear them sawing and hammering every day, and soon he could see the rooms that were being added to the house. There were plumbers and electricians too, and last of all, painters. One of them stopped to buy a peck of corn meal from Mr. Hilton. "Thanksgiving's only two weeks off," he said, "and I want stuffing out of cornbread made from real, sure-enough stone-ground meal."

Mr. Hilton hated to be reminded that Thanksgiving was so near. That was the day he was to move to Atlanta; he'd been trying to put it out of his mind. "When will the new folks be moving in?" he asked.

"The house is ready anytime they are," said the painter, starting out with his bag of meal. Mr. Hilton held the door open and followed him outside. The painter, noticing the chicken across the yard, asked, "Is that your Thanksgiving dinner pecking around out there?"

"It'd make a good one," said Mr. Hilton as the painter got into his panel truck and drove away.

Mr. Hilton called to Wild Wings, "You'd be too old and tough to bake, but you'd make a good stew!" He brought out some cracked corn and threw it into the yard. "Did you hear the man say that the work on the farmhouse is finished?"

The chicken ate the grain as Mr. Hilton continued to talk. "From all that's been added to it, those folks must have a big family. Probably there'll be a houseful of children, and every one of them will be wild as can be! They'll give you a lively chase!" The chicken cocked his head as if he were interested in what Mr. Hilton was saying. "They'll have dogs too, probably a whole pack of them with nothing to do but hunt chickens!" The chicken moved forward as if the thought of wild children and dogs did not bother him.

Then Mr. Hilton said, "Of course, you may not be here

to be bothered by them. I may take you to Atlanta with me, did you know that? My family says I can't go through another winter here alone, and I say you'd be hard put to get through freezing weather if I weren't around to toss you a few scraps or a handful of grain every now and then. But don't worry, we'll be looked after!" Then he laughed, but not as if what he was thinking was really funny. "We'll be kept up and looked after, you and me. So we'll give up our freedom; what's so bad about that?"

Wild Wings turned and walked away. Mr. Hilton closed the mill and went home to fix supper. He thought of eating a dish of cold cereal, which was his usual night meal, but he was especially hungry. Maybe it was the painter's talk about turkey stuffing made from cornbread. His mother used to make cornbread stuffing, and so had Janie. Just thinking about those days put him in the humor for a good meal, so he went into the kitchen and peeled a big potato, scraped three carrots, and chopped an onion. After putting the vegetables in a pot to boil, he decided to make a hoecake to go with them. Even though he ran the gristmill and had all the flour and meal that he wanted, he had bought most of his bread in recent years. But tonight there would be hoecake! He mixed a bit of salt and water with corn meal and poured the mixture into a greased skillet to bake on top of the stove. He would have himself a real feast.

While his supper was cooking, Mr. Hilton sat down in his easy chair in the next room. Soon the water was boiling in the pot and the lid made a cheerful sound as it bounced up and down. He could smell the cornbread batter as it began to dry out. There was something special about the smell of bread baking, even a simple hoecake on top of the stove. He closed his eyes as he thought of kitchen sounds and sights and smells from all the years he had lived in the cottage. He thought about holiday times when he was a boy, and he thought about holiday times when he and Janie were young parents and Mildred and Henry were small.

Memories came back so fast that it was not easy to sort them out. One minute he was thinking about himself as a boy, the next moment he was confusing himself with one of his own children. But always there were good things cooking in the kitchen. Best of all he had liked the sweets. He liked to smell them cooking, and even more, he liked to eat them! He had missed such things in recent years. Somehow store-bought sweets were not as good as homemade ones.

Two hours later, still in his chair, he woke up coughing. The house was filled with smoke. Quickly he dashed into the kitchen and took the pot and skillet outdoors. Everything looked like charcoal. And the pans were a sight; they looked as if molten lava from a volcano had been poured into them. They'd be trouble to clean, he knew, but he'd worry about that later.

As soon as the smoke cleared away, he went back into the kitchen and sat down to a dish of cold cereal.

7

The Trap

THERE was a frost in early November.

Wild Wings had roosted outdoors since early spring, but now he moved to the porch of the cottage. He flew onto the crossbeams at sundown. Once during the night, when Mr. Hilton got up to look for an extra quilt, he heard the chicken shifting from one beam to another.

In the morning, on his way through the grove, Mr. Hilton called to Wild Wings, "You used to stay in the treetops till a hard freeze came along, but now you look for more protection after the first frost! You're not as tough as you once were!" The voice in the back of his head replied, "Neither are you!" He paid no attention to it. Instead, he called to the chicken, "It's just as well that you're going to Atlanta with me!"

Somehow saying it aloud made the decision final. Until then he had not been able to make up his mind, thinking it might be cruel to take the chicken along. An Easter chicken or duck that had been hatched in an incubator and raised in a box might not mind the cramped quarters of a pen, but the mill chicken had known open space all his life. "Well, so have I!" snapped Mr. Hilton. "And what about danger if I'm not here? The fox will come more often, and the hunters will shoot at you! And where would you find spilled corn or wheat if the mill's not running?"

He began to sound angry, as if the chicken were making him mad, and he shook his fist at Wild Wings. Then he stopped, realizing that he was arguing with no one and that he was shaking his fist at the world—at old age, at failing strength and weakened eyesight, and a memory that some-times became confused. It was these things that made him mad, not the chicken, who had paid no attention anyway. He shouted back at Wild Wings, "It's for your own good that I'll take you with me!" He sounded like Mildred. "It's for your own good!" she had said when she had persuaded him to move to the city.

It gave him a sick feeling to think about it, and his stom-ach began to hurt. When he was a boy he had gotten a stomach-ache whenever he knew he had to do something he dreaded. It was the same now.

He wished he hadn't agreed to move on Thanksgiving Day. Why hadn't he held out for Christmas? Because Mil-dred wouldn't hear of it, that was why. She had wanted him to move in October, and they had compromised on Thanksgiving. "I'll send George to get you by noon," she had told him on her last visit. "He and Mavis and the kids are coming over for dinner." George was her oldest son, and it would be nice to see him again. Mr. Hilton looked forward to visiting with his great-grandchildren too. It would be fun—if only he could return home to the mill and the pond and the cottage afterward.

There were no customers that day at the gristmill, so he had plenty of time to think about a way to trap the chicken. A steel trap would break the chicken's leg when it sprang shut, he decided.

What about a wooden trap? As a boy he had made traps that he called rabbit boxes. Long and narrow, they had looked like small crates, and nothing caught in them was harmed.

Mr. Hilton laughed when he remembered the time he had caught a skunk. He was in the fifth grade, and one of his traps was in a clump of weeds out near the road. He always checked his traps in the afternoons, but one morning when the school bus was a few minutes late, he had run over to see if anything was in the trap. Sure enough the door was closed, and when he reached into the dark trap, thinking he would pull out a rabbit, a skunk sprayed him. It scared him at first, and then he had thought it was funny.

He had turned the skunk loose and was resetting the trap when the bus came along. The driver let him on, but the other riders threatened to throw him off. Finally they settled for opening all the windows, and at school his teacher opened every window of the classroom. Even then, she suggested that maybe he'd like to play outside for a while—an extended recess she had called it. Mr. Hilton, who had never cared much about book learning, anyway, remembered it as the best day he'd ever spent in school.

But Wild Wings was too smart to walk into a wooden trap. Finally Mr. Hilton decided that a simple wire hook like the one the farmer's wife had used for catching the fryers would be best. For added strength he would use two coathangers instead of one. He could not get close enough to Wild Wings in the daytime to use the hook, but he could catch him at night. The fox had almost caught the chicken, and surely Wild Wings would trust Mr. Hilton to get nearer to him than he had the fox.

Mr. Hilton decided that he would start going onto the porch every night. He would go nearer Wild Wings on each visit, and gradually the chicken would become accustomed to his being there. Then, on Thanksgiving eve, he would make the catch; it was simple.

The first night that Mr. Hilton went onto the porch, Wild Wings was frightened. He jumped from one crossbeam to another, and Mr. Hilton was afraid that the chicken was going to fly into the darkness. "It's only me," Mr. Hilton said softly, and went back into the cottage.

The next night he stayed longer, and on the third night Wild Wings did not appear to even notice him.

The next morning Mr. Hilton set up a stepladder on the porch. It was an old one that had been under the house for years. Mildred had almost fainted the time she caught

him climbing on it to saw off an oak limb that brushed
against the house when the wind blew. "Don't *ever* get back
on that ladder to saw off a limb!" she pleaded. "It's rickety!
It's wobbly! It's dangerous! What if you should fall?" He
knew the answer to "What if you should fall?" He might
break a hip or a leg and have to lie in bed all the time. Well,
Mildred wasn't with him now, and anyway, he had promised her that he wouldn't climb the ladder to saw off limbs.
He hadn't made a bargain about any other use of it.

At dusk Wild Wings flew onto the porch railing. He
looked at the ladder without going nearer. At last he flew
back into the yard and spent the night in a tulip tree. But
the next afternoon he returned to the porch and flew from
the railing to one of the crossbeams to roost. The following
afternoon he flew onto the top of the ladder and then to a
crossbeam. That night Mr. Hilton, in his visit to the porch,
took a step up the ladder. The next night he took two steps,
and the ladder swayed slightly. "She's right!" he thought,

remembering Mildred. "It could be dangerous! But I'll be careful."

He went back into the house and began to twist two coat-hanger wires together. With pliers he bent the ends of them to make a hook the width of the chicken's leg, just above the foot. Then he flared out the end of the hook so that it would slip easily into position and hold the chicken firmly.

On the Sunday before Thanksgiving Mr. Hilton went onto the porch and halfway up the ladder. He shined his flashlight onto the chicken. "From here," he said softly, "I could reach you with the wire just fine!" Wild Wings did not move. "It's trading on your trust in me that I'll be able to catch you," said Mr. Hilton, as if he were apologizing. "But I've told you before: it's for your own good."

8

The Catch

ON Monday morning a moving van came down the road. Wild Wings was scratching for bugs near a big rock; he looked up as the van drove into the yard of the farmhouse. Mr. Hilton saw the van from the doorway of the gristmill and came outside. "Yep, they're moving in!" he called to the chicken.

Wild Wings went on scratching, but Mr. Hilton stood and watched the unloading. Somehow the house looked different to him when he knew furniture was inside it. It was nice to think of people living nearby.

Later in the morning another van arrived, and just after

noon two pickup trucks unloaded at the house. After a while the vans and the pickup trucks left, and nothing stirred at the farmhouse except a denim jacket that one of the moving men had left on a gatepost. It flapped about in the breeze like a flag, as if it were proclaiming that once again the house was to be lived in. Soon the breeze died away and even the denim jacket was still.

In the late afternoon a station wagon and a car drove into the yard. Mr. Hilton wished they hadn't parked so near the farmhouse. He would have liked a better look at the passengers. A man got out of the car, he was sure of that, and a boy. He could not tell for certain how many passengers were in the station wagon. A woman had driven it, and there were children—and maybe a dog.

When he went onto the porch that night and climbed partway up the stepladder, he said to the chicken, "Our neighbors have a houseful of children and dogs! What do you think of that?" Wild Wings, so accustomed to Mr. Hilton's visits, did not act as if he had heard.

On Tuesday Mr. Hilton did not see the new people. The children were indoors or in school, he supposed. The car was gone all day, but the station wagon went in and out of the driveway a number of times. It was the same on Wednesday, Thanksgiving eve. Mr. Hilton wished he could meet his neighbors, even though he would be around only one more night. He would enjoy knowing what sort of folks would be here when he was gone. Maybe he should go to the farmhouse and introduce himself to them. But they were probably busy getting settled. He didn't want to bother them, so he went home and ate supper early. Afterward he went to bed, reminding himself that he had to get up before daybreak if he was to catch the chicken.

He woke before dawn. The little clock on the mantelpiece was striking, and his first thought was that he must be sure to take the clock to Atlanta. The sound of it would be company for him—a reminder of home.

He dressed quickly and took the flashlight and hook and went onto the porch. "It's just me," he said softly. "I'm

coming up the ladder one last time. I'm coming to get you!"
He was less steady than usual, and one of his feet almost
slipped when the third rung of the ladder twisted slightly.
For a moment he was afraid he would lose his balance. He
must not fall, he kept telling himself, but the more he said
it the shakier he felt and the more wobbly the ladder
seemed. "There's plenty of time," he said, waiting a few
moments before easing up another step . . . and then another.

Within reach of the chicken he shined his flashlight on
Wild Wings. "It's just me," he whispered, moving the
hook forward . . . carefully . . . cautiously . . . "Easy does
it now!" The hook was just above the foot of the chicken,
who stood up but did not seem alarmed. Then Mr. Hilton
gave a yank.

Wild Wings was pulled from his perch. He squawked
loudly and flapped his wings mightily. He stayed in the air,
although one leg was caught. Mr. Hilton held firmly to
the wire and started to climb down.

It was the third rung of the ladder that was at fault. It gave way, and he fell. One foot touched a lower rung but slid from it. He dropped the flashlight and desperately tried to break his fall by clinging to the side of the ladder with his free hand. Splinters from the wood tore into his flesh. He landed on his feet with such force that his knees gave way, and he sprawled on the floor, gripping the wire. The chicken flapped his wings frantically. Mr. Hilton pulled Wild Wings to him.

Holding the chicken by both legs, wings brushing against his face as they beat the air, Mr. Hilton crawled across the floor. Pulling himself forward on his elbows, he got to the edge of the porch. After resting a few seconds he managed to sit on the top step. His legs hurt, but he was glad to be able to move them.

"You don't know when to give up, do you?" he said to the chicken, pressing him against his chest to stop the wings from flapping. At last Wild Wings was still and quiet. Mr. Hilton could feel the chicken's heart beating . . . pounding urgently. "In all the years you've been alive, this is the first time you've been held captive," he said, speaking softly in an attempt to calm Wild Wings. "But don't worry, we'll go to the city, you and me." The heartbeat continued at such a furious rate that it all but shook the steps. Lowering Wild Wings to his lap, Mr. Hilton wondered if chickens, like people, had heart attacks. So fierce was the pounding against his chest that it scared him, and then he realized that Wild Wings was in his lap and the runaway heartbeat was his own. He grew even more frightened, and his heart beat faster. "My time has come!" he said as he slumped forward, losing consciousness.

When he opened his eyes a moment later he was bent over, his hands held loosely in his lap. Wild Wings was still in his lap, and he seemed calmer.

Mr. Hilton's own heart had slowed so much that he wasn't sure it still beat at all. He sat quietly and stared into the darkness until day began to break. Talking to the chicken, he whispered, "You'd rather stay here and take your chances, wouldn't you?" Hesitantly, as if he were not sure what was best, he continued, "Well, all right then. Let them coop me up if they want to, but you remain free!"

Wild Wings didn't move. "Did you die instead of me?" asked Mr. Hilton, not raising his voice. Louder he added, "I said, 'You're on your own!' Now get!" He nudged the chicken with one hand, and Wild Wings gave a start. Finding himself free, he fluttered to the ground and ran, staggering at first, across the yard. Gradually he regained his balance, and at the edge of the yard he flew over a grape arbor and into a sycamore tree in the grove.

In the first rays of Thanksgiving sunshine Mr. Hilton watched the chicken fly from one branch to another. Wild Wings flew higher and higher, deeper and deeper into the grove, and as Mr. Hilton watched he forgot that he was tired or that he might be seriously hurt. He forgot that he was an old man who was giving up the work that he had done all his life. He forgot that he would be leaving his cottage, the only home he had ever known, in a few hours.

He watched the chicken's flight through the treetops and felt better than he had in years. He felt young again . . . and strong . . . and best of all, free! His spirits were lifted each time the chicken flew higher, with wings flapping as if they had never, even for a brief moment, been pinned together.

When the chicken was out of sight, Mr. Hilton sat staring in the direction in which Wild Wings had flown. Gradually the good feeling began to drain away, and he felt chilly. There was an east wind blowing that he had not even noticed earlier, and he shivered as once again he felt like an old man.

9

The Neighbors

IT took Mr. Hilton half an hour to remove all the splinters. Then he made breakfast. Afterward he went to the mill. It would be his last time. No customers would come on a holiday, but still, he wanted to be there. It gave him something to do, something to keep his mind off the pain in his hand where the splinters had ripped into it. Also, it kept him from thinking about the soreness in his legs and back.

He remembered a November day in school a long time ago—the year he was in the fourth grade. His teacher, after talking about Thanksgiving and how it started, asked the boys and girls to make lists of everything for which they were especially thankful. His list had been: "Coconut pie, chocolate pie, lemon pie, raisin pie, apple pie, and pecan pie." Some of his classmates had called him Pie for a long time afterward. Well, he still liked pie, but if he were drawing up a list today, he would be especially thankful that he had not broken any bones when he fell from the ladder. Also, he was thankful that he had changed his mind about caging the chicken. He went outside and looked around but did not see Wild Wings.

Back in the mill he swept the floor and gave the place a good cleaning. In one corner he found a small bag of corn. He threw the grains into the yard. "Wild Wings," he called, "wherever you are, here's a final feast!"

He went back into the mill and continued his cleaning, patting each piece of machinery as if it were an old friend. By late morning he knew that it was time to lock up. On a piece of cardboard he lettered a sign, "GONE OUT OF BUSI-NESS," which he hung on the door. In the yard he turned and looked back at it. He hesitated, started away again, and then stopped once more. He went back to the sign and added "TEMPORARILY."

"Who knows but what one of my grandsons will reopen it someday?" he said aloud. "Or maybe one of my grand-daughters." He had heard recently about a woman who ran a gristmill in the northern part of the state. Women did all sorts of jobs now.

At the cottage he got out a big basket his wife had used for hanging out clothes. It would hold the belongings he wanted to take with him. There was no suitcase because he had never needed one.

A few clothes went into the basket, along with his tooth-brush and razor. He looked around to see what else he would take. The picture of Janie, he wanted it with him. It had been taken at a carnival when they were courting, and it was the only picture he had of her. "That was a long time ago," he thought, gently pulling the picture from where it had been stuck all these years into the edge of the mirror over the chest of drawers. On top of the chest there were snapshots of Mildred and Henry when they were in school, and his grandchildren, who were now grown up, and their sons and daughters—his great-grandchildren.

All the pictures went into a shoebox, which he put into the basket. Then he dusted off the little clock. He put it into the basket and was packing underwear around it when someone knocked at the door.

It would be George, coming for him. Maybe some of his kids had come with him. The few times George had been here in recent years he had come without his children. They'd always been at ball practice or scout meetings or baton twirling lessons or something—but maybe they had come along this time. Mr. Hilton hoped so, and he hoped they'd want to see the mill. It would give him a reason to go there another time. "Come in!" he called, expecting George to enter, but when the door did not open he went to see who was there.

A woman and a girl stood just outside. "We're your new neighbors," said the woman. "I'm Irene Gresham, and this is my daughter Kelly."

Mr. Hilton invited them inside, but they declined. "We're not making a real visit this time," said the woman. "We left our Thanksgiving dinner cooking, but the day is so beautiful that we decided to get outside for a few minutes, anyway."

Kelly, who looked to be around twelve years old, handed Mr. Hilton a small brown bag. "We brought you some cookies," she said, smiling shyly. "They're oatmeal."

"My favorite kind!" said Mr. Hilton.

"Today's the first chance we've had to try out our new stove with cookies," said Mrs. Gresham. "They're not the best ever, but we'll do better next time!"

"I'm afraid I won't be here next time," said Mr. Hilton, "but these look fine to me." Then he explained that he was moving to Atlanta.

"Can we be of help to you in any way?" asked Mrs. Gresham.

"No, I suppose not," said Mr. Hilton. "But thank you." Then he glanced toward the mill. Through the grove he saw Wild Wings busily scratching at the corn that he had thrown out earlier. "Come to think of it," he said, "maybe there is *one* thing you could do." He pointed toward the mill. "Do you see that chicken?"

Mrs. Gresham and Kelly said they could see it clearly, and Mr. Hilton continued, "Well, if we have a tough winter and things stay frozen-over for any length of time, maybe you'd throw him a few scraps along till spring. Then he can make out all right."

Kelly said enthusiastically, "I'll look after him!"

She sounded so excited that Mr. Hilton added, "But

don't try to make a pet out of him. He values his freedom."

"She'll enjoy him on his own terms," said her mother. "Kelly's always been the one in our family to feed the birds and squirrels, and she doesn't have to tame something to care about it."

"I'll leave food for the chicken every day," said Kelly. "I'll be good to him, and I'll keep Hal and Suzy and Judge away from him."

"Hal and Suzy are Kelly's younger brother and sister," explained Mrs. Gresham, "and Judge is their dog."

"And I'll keep 'em from chasing the chicken!" promised Kelly.

Mr. Hilton laughed. "Oh, don't be *that* good to him! Don't take the risk out of living!"

Mrs. Gresham smiled. "It's too late, anyway," she said, motioning toward the mill. The boy and the girl and their dog had discovered Wild Wings and were chasing him across the clearing. He flew into the mulberries, and they went in after him. Wild Wings dashed out the back of the thicket and ran along the edge of the pond to the narrow place near the dam. From there he flew to the other side.

Mr. Hilton, Mrs. Gresham, and Kelly watched Hal, Suzy, and Judge tromp about in the briers, searching for the strange, gray chicken they had chased into the thicket. From a pine tree across the pond Wild Wings was watching too.

ABOUT THE AUTHOR

ROBERT BURCH was born in Fayette County, Georgia, and grew up there with seven brothers and sisters. Despite the economic hardships of the nineteen thirties, he relishes many happy memories of those years. Mr. Burch draws on his childhood experiences for background material in his books, but, he says, "the incidents come from my imagination." Georgia is the setting for many of his popular books for young people, including *Queenie Peavy*, an ALA Notable Book, *Renfroe's Christmas*, *Doodle and the Go-cart*, and *Hut School and the Wartime Home-Front Heroes*.

Robert Burch now lives in the house in which he spent his youth, and he devotes most of his time to writing—the career he says he "would not trade for any other."

ABOUT THIS BOOK

The text type used in *Two That Were Tough* is Caslon Old Face and the display type faces are Caslon Openface and Bullfinch Old Style. The art work was done in pencil with watercolor washes. Printed by offset, the book is bound in paper and cloth over boards.